ELOQUENT YEARS OF SILENCE

SILENCE

John Travis

PRESS

Published by Vulpine Press in the United Kingdom in 2021

ISBN: 978-1-83919-381-1

www.vulpine-press.com

1

"Don't be silly," he kept hearing Wendy saying over and over. "You'll be doing us a huge favour – as long as you don't mind what we were talking about earlier."

Laying in bed, he replayed the conversation he'd had with the Masons earlier in the evening, searching for any doubt in their words.

"Perhaps if I paid some bills for you…"

Wendy and Graeme exchanged exasperated glances. "Why? We're not going to be paying board with Wendy's mother in Auckland, are we?" Graeme told him. "At least I hope not."

"Look, we want you to house sit, that's all," Wendy said, ignoring Graeme's remark. "You need somewhere to live, we don't want to be burgled. There's been enough of that around here. Are – are you sure you're okay about next door?"

Bundrick was aware of what had happened to Moffatt and was both intrigued and appalled in equal measure. The end house had lain empty for six months, but it didn't stop the talk. "I'll check it every day. And if I see any kids inside, I'll call the police," he promised.

"Well, that's that then," Graeme said, fixing them another drink. "We leave for the airport at two on Friday morning. Move in any time after that."

As he left, Wendy gave Bundrick his customary hug. "You always look so worried," she told him as he put on his jacket. "Everything will be fine. Enjoy it, you'll have the whole place to yourself. *Relax.*"

Bundrick knew she was right; for the first time in his thirty-five years he'd have the run of a house to himself, instead of a poky flat or bedsit.

It had to be better than this place, he thought, laying there in the cold darkness in his scratchy, undersized bed. As if on cue, a stereo boomed from a downstairs flat. He looked across at his digital clock: nearly quarter to two. Wendy was right – he should relax. How many times had she said it to him? But how could he ask her how to do it?

As someone else began crashing around below he thought again about Wendy asking if he was okay with what'd happened to their neighbour.

It had happened before Graeme and Wendy moved into the terrace, and by the time they knew the story it was too late to do anything about it. As it turned out they really liked the house, despite the fact that Matthew Moffatt's last few weeks next door were still the cause of much gossip around the town (and for the first few weeks after they'd moved in, sightseers), which was only now beginning to die down.

The story went that Moffatt's nearest neighbours at the time (the house the Masons now lived in was empty at that point), the Wallaces had gone to complain about the smell coming from the end house. Knocking at Moffatts door there was no reply, but they heard what sounded like a cat inside, although they were sure the old man didn't have one. A few days later when they tried again with the same result, they called the council.

When the door was forced they found what was left of Moffatt in the lounge, his badly decomposed body slumped in a green armchair (the rumour about the corpse being half liquefied Bundrick put down to mischievous gossip), and the room overrun with fungus which had evidently seeped in through the wall after a prolonged period of heavy rain. At the inquest it was ruled that Moffatt had been dead for approximately four to six weeks – during which time, the Wallaces insisted they'd heard voices coming from inside the house. The voices were put down to a combination of the strange way sound carried through the terraces, and the probability of them having heard children playing directly behind the house in the disused woodyard. The inquest also heard that Moffatt, a widower of twenty years, had become more and more withdrawn and uncommunicative in the months leading up to his death, refusing offers of help from the Wallaces, who'd used to check on him two or three times a week to see if he was all right.

In the flat below Bundrick's the stereo was switched off, the booming replaced by loud, angry voices. Closing his eyes, Bundrick tried to heed Wendy's advice by taking deep breaths, but his pulse continued to motor, and sleep was long incoming.

2

By Friday evening Bundrick felt calmer and found he was looking forward to moving into Wendy and Graeme's. Returning to his flat after work, he put the rumours to one side and went straight to Barrett to pay off what he owed in rent. Handing the money over to the older man, Bundrick shuddered as the greasy hand snatched it from his fingers, and again as he felt that large leathery face staring down at him, making him feel, as always, like a naughty schoolboy. He'd tried telling himself that Barrett treated everybody like this, but he knew it was a bit worse for him. They'd never seen eye to eye.

In the front room, Bundrick's bags had been packed since Wednesday. He went through the formality of checking the other rooms, anyway, knowing the only things left were things that'd been there when he'd arrived eighteen months earlier. Staring at the sofa, its colour faded by the sun, he thought of his time there.

Eighteen months. It's like I've never been here. Nothing belongs to me – the furniture, the television, the curtains, the fridge. I arrived with four holdalls and I'm leaving with four. I've made no impression whatsoever. It's like I'm invisible.

But deep down this was the way he wanted it; it meant he couldn't ruin any more lives. It was only every once in a while, a part of him wondered what it would be like to mean something to somebody again.

There was also the question of what would happen in eight weeks' time. He swore to himself he wouldn't end up in a place like this again, but the fact remained that in two months he'd likely be in the same position he was in now.

Taking the bags out to the car, he heard scrabbling noises coming from the downstairs flat and realised he couldn't get out quickly enough. Looking into the rooms a final time, he turned his back and went downstairs.

As he did, Barrett and his greasy, dyed-black widow's peak appeared around a door.

"Keys," he snapped.

Holding the keys at arm's length but still beyond Barrett's reach, Bundrick let them drop to the floor where they tinkled on the concrete. Before Barrett could respond Bundrick marched out of the hall, slamming the door as hard as he could.

With the rush-hour traffic long gone, the roads were pretty quiet. To his left the ugly detached houses built in the 60's and 70's bobbled up and down as the car went over the potholes in the road, occasionally replaced by fragile-looking plants hanging over their garden walls.

Stuck behind the same car for nearly ten minutes now, its MEA registration plate was engraved in Bundrick's memory. When its driver looked at him in the mirror again, he hoped they didn't think he was following them. Indicating left to turn into the estate he wasn't surprised when the other car did the same. Slowing for the terrace, he hoped it would take the next left, but it turned into the cobbled terrace too. Perhaps he should explain who he was and where he was going.

As he was opening his door, Bundrick saw the driver of the car was coming towards him.

"I thought it was you behind me."

A tallish woman with brown wavy hair smiled down at him. She seemed oddly familiar, making him even more uneasy.

"I've seen you visiting Graeme and Wendy before. I thought it was you then." She smiled at his puzzlement. "You don't remember me, Jim?"

Bundrick's chest felt as heavy as lead.

"Rebecca – we hung about together, a load of us in a group. We were in the same classes for a while, too."

He found himself being dragged back to events he didn't want to think about. But then he remembered who she was, and that she was okay. Seeing a younger version of the woman in front of him, he smiled back at her.

"I remember you – Rebecca Hudson. How are you?"

"Rebecca Wallace now. Fine." She looked at him carefully, unsure what to say as unpleasant memories began to surface. "How about you?"

With equal care he told her why he was here. She nodded.

"Wendy told me they had a house sitter lined up. Well, you'll have to pop in and we can talk about old times." The words were hardly out of her mouth when she regretted them.

"Yes. Yes. That'd be nice."

"Well, I'll let you get in," she said after an uncomfortable pause. Glad it was over, Bundrick began taking the bags from his boot.

"Bye Jim," she called out.

"Bye." Was that a look of pity in her eyes?

Flipping the keys from his pocket, they dropped on the cobbles, the sound strangely similar to the noise the keys had made on Barrett's floor. Picking them up quickly, he opened the door and dumped the bags inside.

Within the hour he had his feet up on the sofa and a pot of coffee at his side. Forgetting the scene outside he sank into the house's quietness. After the flat, the silence was astonishing. It was almost physical: he imagined himself sinking into it, and the further into it he went the less inclined he was to come out.

I've escaped, he thought. A part of him couldn't take it in. *I've actually escaped.*

It wasn't long before his eyelids began to close.

3

Bundrick woke up on Saturday morning shivering but feeling freer than he had in years. He got changed in *his* bedroom, the spare one; the main one was still the Mason's, even if they weren't here. He wouldn't have felt comfortable taking it for himself.

After getting washed, he went downstairs and made coffee. Looking through to the living room, the morning's paper leaned against the front door like an upturned V, beneath it a jumble of white envelopes and cellophane. Taking them through to the kitchen, he put them on the table in a neat pile.Sunlight poured through the glass kitchen door, staining the table a rich gold as twisted fingers of smoke curled up from his coffee cup before evaporating. Letting out a contented sigh, he decided today would be a lazy day, a day to get the feel of the place. Recalling a less unpleasant childhood memory he smiled.

As a child going to school on the bus, he'd passed row upon row of weather-blackened Victorian terraces. Looking into their upstairs windows from the top deck, he'd always thought there was something romantic about them, all those people living side by side like that. And now here he was, actually *in* one of them. Surprised at this whimsical turn of mood, he found his smile broaden.

Later, clutching a cup of hot coffee in his hands, Bundrick tip-toed almost reverently through the house, studying each of the rooms; the living room was small and cosy, despite only the door and a drop of six inches separating him from the street outside. Its walls were a warm pastel orange, with two small bookcases sitting either side of the fireplace. The kitchen was the largest room in the house ("Big enough to hold a dance in," Graeme had told him), with all its appliances back against the walls. A large dining table occupied the centre of the room, and a small door in the right-hand wall presumably led to a broom cupboard.

At the top of the gleaming varnished staircase, two further steps on the right led to the front bedroom. Wincing at the bright purple walls, he felt even happier he'd taken the bedroom opposite, which had the bathroom next to it, both rooms overlooking the alley leading to the next terrace row, its ancient brick walls like a reflection. Over to the right what remained of the old woodyard was now little more than a sludgy dumping ground.

Fancying a walk, Bundrick grabbed his jacket and skipped down the stairs, and out through the living room. As he was putting the key in his pocket a noise to his left made him jump.

Bouncing along in the autumnal breeze, a red tin can clunked across the cobbles, only stopping when it hit the wall next to the house. Next to the can a fast-food carton looked ready to pounce, its lid opening and closing like a set of gnashing jaws.

The street was empty. About to turn away, something at ground level glistened, catching his eye. Seeing the few inches of glass rising above the pavement, he realized the small door in the kitchen must lead to the basement Graham had mentioned, not a cupboard.

Stepping back, he looked at Moffatt's house. Not that there was much to see – the windows were covered in thick grease which even the sun couldn't pierce. But it was comforting to see that all the panes were intact.

Looking at the upstairs windows of each house in turn, presumably all master bedrooms, it occurred to Bundrick that it was like a dormitory for adults, each room separated only by a foot of brick and a different set of curtains, apart from the end house whose windows were empty.

His gaze kept going back to the end house, a poor relation stuck on the end as an afterthought, almost invisible. Is that the way Moffatt had wanted it? It occurred to him then that he wasn't thinking about Moffatt, but himself. *Yes, this would be the perfect place,* he thought bitterly, *tucked away at the end of a street within a street, a street that nobody had any cause to visit.*

Shocked at this sudden burst of anger, he looked around again to see if he was being watched. Seeing he wasn't, he went over to the house anyway. He had to think about living somewhere. He'd seen other terraces for sale in the area; it didn't have to be one that was tucked away. After checking the door was properly secure, he went to the wall.

Between it and the house was a gap of maybe six to eight inches, running from front to back; at the far side, the next row of houses was visible. He noticed the woodyard wall appeared to be at an angle, bending slightly inwards; the reason, a pulpy mixture of rainwater, mud and trapped leaves stuck between the two walls like a layer of thick black mulch that was impossible to clear away.

Standing back, he became aware of a metallic clanging behind him, one beat dragging slightly behind the other like church bells, *clang-clang, clang-clang,* the rhythm occasionally broken by voices as it thrummed along the wall.

Checking his own door again he left the terrace. Heading right towards the main road, he decided he'd double back on himself past the remaining terraces and come back past the woodyard.

The relative silence was broken by two cars racing each other on the main road; as they passed, a woman with a pram put her head down. Weak sunlight glinted on the windows to his right, but the window of the newsagents was so full of advertisements for vapes and soft drinks that he couldn't see the glass. On the other side of the road, an entire row of one-storey shops looked deserted until an elderly man and woman hobbled out of the betting shop and went into the butcher's next door.

After passing a disused railway bridge, the numbers of houses decreased. Most were detached and squalid, a stop-start procession of grey brick walls and muddy gardens filled with junk; shroud-like net curtains hung in the filthy windows. A knot of teenagers across the road scowled as he went by. He did his best to make himself invisible but the more he tried the more conspicuous he seemed to be, his walking becoming self-conscious. Tripping over his feet a few minutes later, a second group of youths standing around a bicycle as if for heat cheered. He breathed a sigh of relief when he saw the next turning up ahead.

Then he noticed the clanging again, until an out-of-date sports car shot past him crammed full of grinning teenagers and momentarily blotted it out. Avoiding the looks from the teenagers, he feigned interest in what was across the road. But realising what it was – a derelict public house – he soon forgot the teenagers, and a small current of excitement ran through his veins.

11

Before he had a chance to change his mind, he was standing in what must have been the pub's car park, his feet grinding in the dust. Looking up he took in the building slowly, savouring it as he always did on such occasions.

Despite being defaced with every kind of graffiti imaginable, "The Ratcatcher's Inn" still boasted a small plaque bearing its name above the door. At ground level, randomly applied panels of wood covered the window frames; above, several contained slivers of glass that protruded like teeth, angled in at each other from the four corners of their frames.

As ever, his excitement was evenly balanced with the memories he tried his best to block. It was macabre, he knew; he also knew that part of the allure of the Mason's property was that it was next door to an abandoned house. There was a perverse kind of security in dilapidated buildings, like a promise of ultimate safety.

It was, like his feelings towards old houses in general, a romantic notion: the older the building, the safer it became, no matter how derelict it was. Chances were, it had had everything thrown at it over the years and yet somehow had survived and was now unable to be hurt anymore. He liked that idea.

Despite the cars parked in driveways along the roads, the three streets Bundrick could see into were deserted. Three strides took him to the pub's door, and it was open. As he was about to go inside, he noticed the wood panels on the bottom two windows on the right were slightly off-kilter. He peered between them to check the room was empty.

As his eyes adjusted to the greyness, various odd shapes floated up before him. He had the impression of being at the bottom of

12

the ocean; everything looked as if it was coated in silt. A few up-ended chairs and tables were covered in balls of fur, surrounded by crushed beer cans. In contrast the back wall was so black it looked like everything apart from the bricks had been ripped out. A quaint painted tile beside the next window informed him this had been The Snug. The foundations of bolted-down seats were still visible in the dust. On the far side of the room, another of the boards had slipped; he could see right through the building to the empty street beyond.

Slowly opening the door, a bit wider, a shaft of grey light appeared two floors above him through the scorched beams of the floor and the brittle timbers of the roof. Among the criss-cross of charred boards, he spotted a small, ball-like mixture of twigs and salt-and-pepper feathers; he wondered how birds managed to nest in such peculiar places.Luckily, the hole in the floor above was quite small and the rest of it looked intact. He'd be okay as long as he was careful. Beside the first flight of stairs, two doors lead left and right. He looked back a final time to check the area was still clear.

Just as he was about to step over the threshold, he heard a noise from inside, and something dropped from the ceiling. At first, he thought it was dust; instead, a bloom of feathers fluttered down towards him. An unpleasant image tried to form in his head, but he wouldn't let it through. *Just a bird*, he told himself. He took a step inside.

Directly above he heard shuffling, followed by muffled voices. Panicked, Bundrick jerked back against the door, its hollow thud echoing in the stillness. The voices continued, but now seemed louder, closer. He had to get away.

He managed to get across the road seconds before a small van sped around the corner, the face inside turning to look at him. Looking back towards the pub uneasily he saw that nothing had followed him out, and nobody was looking at him from the windows of the nearby houses.

Walking away, he took deep breaths to calm himself, annoyed that he never learned. He shouldn't have gone near. It was probably being used by drug addicts, or squatters. Graeme had warned him about various places in the area, but he'd been so keen to leave his flat he hadn't listened. It never occurred to him he'd swapped like for like. But he mustn't think like that. It was a nice area, compared to where he'd come from.

Opposite the woodyard now, he heard the clanging again, close to a section of the uneven wall running along its edge. He could make out something else too; a dusty clacking, like someone chipping away at something.

Stopping at a section of the wall where the hedge was taller than the brick, Bundrick looked into the yard and saw damp lengths of timber overgrown with weeds and flowers, surrounded by litter thrown over the hedges.

Moving away, he realised that the higher the wall was the louder the clanging became. A few seconds later he saw what was causing it: straddled either side of the wall, two youths sat with their backs to each other, both armed with lump hammers which were swinging back and forth like pendulums, knocking great chunks out of the wall and into the yard. He supposed it must be safer to demolish the wall this way than to close off the road. As he passed the youths, he was sure the hammering slowed down.

Quickening his pace, he only stopped to avoid stepping on a black lump on the pavement a few feet away.

The crow was huge, its talons pointing at the sky as the breeze ruffled its greasy feathers. Staring at it intently, he wondered how it had died; it didn't have any feathers missing, and there was no sign of injury. And he doubted a cat could've tackled something so big without getting its eyes gouged out. Looking around, there were no trees close enough for it to have fallen from; and it was absurd to think it could've died falling off the wall. Crows brought bad luck; and after what had happened at "The Ratcatcher's Inn" it felt doubly ominous.

Rushing home, it was as though the clanking of the hammers kept pace with him. Harder than he needed to, he slammed the door shut behind him.

4

Putting his car keys on the table, Terry Wallace turned to his wife and said, "Our new neighbour – does he have a permanently worried expression on his face?"

Rebecca smiled at him. "Yes, he lives on his nerves. Why?"

"I think I've just seen him," he put his coat on the rack in the kitchen, "down near that old pub. Why, what does he have to be worried about?"

"He was the same in school," she called out. "Surprised he wanted to move in round here, to be honest."

"Why's that?"

"Well, after what happened at the end there. Not unless he doesn't know. It'd put anyone off, wouldn't it?"

Terry put his head round the kitchen door, knowing her tone. "But there's more to it than that," he said.

"Yes, there is," she said with a sigh. Pecking him on the cheek she told him she'd see him later.

"You know, Wendy asked me to keep an eye on the place. I thought it sounded a bit odd at the time," Terry said, rubbing at his chin.

"I'll tell you about it later," she told him, opening the door.

5

After his walk on Saturday, Bundrick didn't leave the house again until Monday morning. The weather was on the change, and besides, he liked the quiet; it was nice not to be bothered with noisy neighbours, or people traipsing through the door every five minutes. He felt safe.

The time passed slowly, as if at half speed while the world outside rushed ever onward. He went through Graeme's collection of films, most of them black and white, which suited him – the world seemed a less complicated place in old films. Then he read a bit, selecting books at random from the shelves downstairs and the ones in his room, reading passages at random, briefly inhabiting a different world in each book before moving onto the next.

On Sunday he contemplated another walk. The church was only five minutes away and he doubted he'd be hassled by youths on street corners. Remembering "The Ratcatcher's Inn", he decided to stay put. It wasn't until the evening he remembered he hadn't looked in the basement yet. He decided to do that tomorrow when he got in from work.

That night he had difficulty sleeping. He didn't want to go back to work. Then there was the keening sound outside which meant he'd had to close the window, making the room muggy; it was just a cat on the prowl, no doubt, but better to be safe than sorry. As he was finally dropping off, the cat seemed extremely close; half asleep, he wondered if someone had let it in next door, momentarily forgetting the house was empty.

Next day at work the rumours persisted: the factory was in some kind of trouble because a big order had been cancelled. Keeping his head down, Bundrick got on with his work and pushed the idea aside. He was irritable from lack of sleep and left as soon as his shift ended. As he did someone shouted out behind him. But he was sure it couldn't have been for him.

After ordering a takeaway from the Chinese across from the terraces he popped into the local pub for a quick pint. As he was gulping the drink at the bar, he felt eyes watching him from the other side.

"Hello again."

"Rebecca," he said, after taking another long gulp. "Just finished work."

"I've just started," she said back. "How are you settling in?"

"Fine. Didn't sleep well last night, though. There was a cat prowling around somewhere."

"You heard it as well?" She rubbed at a few glasses. "Terry thinks it sounds more like a baby crying but there aren't any around here."

Swallowing the last of his pint, Bundrick said goodbye and collected his takeaway. Unpacking the cartons onto plates (a luxury he doubted he'd ever get used to), he caught himself bolting down the food the way he'd bolted his drink. With the day he'd had at work he really should try and relax. When he'd been looking through the books over the weekend, he'd seen one in the spare room, about relaxation through hypnotism. "Wendy and her hocus-pocus books," Graeme had once said to him. Still, maybe he could try it. It appeared to work for Wendy.

Just as he was about to go through to the living room, he caught sight of the red light on the answering machine. Pushing the play button, a gruff, breathy voice spoke amid the echo of heavy machinery.

"Jim, it's Dave Hargreaves. I tried to get you as you left but you didn't hear me. I need to speak to you. I'll be here until eight. Bye." When his voice disappeared, a bland female one informed him the call had come in five minutes before he'd got back. His skin began to tingle.

He tried going back to his meal, but it was useless. Picking up the receiver, he pressed redial.

"Hargreaves."

"Hello Dave. Jim Bundrick."

"Ah."

The long pause that followed told him everything he needed to know. His stomach seemed to shrink to the size of a clenched fist.

"You're laying me off, aren't you?"

"Jim, I'm sorry," Hargreaves said. "I really didn't want to have to do this over the phone…"

"How long?" Bundrick asked blankly, staring at the wall.

Hargreaves' sigh crackled down the receiver. "Might only be a couple of weeks."

"But it might not."

"Look, Jim, I'm surprised it's taken so long. There's been talk for weeks, you'll have heard it yourself." He had, but he'd blanked it out, which usually seemed the best way. He hadn't even told the

Masons in case they'd changed their mind about letting him stay there.

As Hargreaves continued apologising Bundrick stared at the half-eaten meal on the coffee table. He'd eat it later cold, he decided. It wasn't the end of the world, he had savings – it wasn't as if he had anything to spend his money on, anyway. And he didn't have to worry about rent for a while. And it might only be a few weeks–

"Jim? Jim, you still there?"

"Hmm? Yes. Yes, I'm still here."

"Look. I'm sorry, I really am. But with any luck you'll be back before you know it."

"I know. Bye." Putting the phone down, he started to cough. The deep breaths he took didn't help. Rushing to the bathroom he retched over the sink. When his meal came back it felt like fire surging from his body.

Wiping his mouth and face with a wet flannel, he went back downstairs and scraped the plate into the bin. Opening one of his holdalls, he took out a bottle of scotch and emptied four inches into a tumbler.

Later, when the fire of the whisky began to override the fire of the bile, he noticed the same noise he'd heard last night, again seemingly very close. Half a bottle of scotch later he couldn't decide if the noises were coming from outside the house or from inside himself.

6

The door opened with a click and Rebecca sighed noisily.

"Have you cleaning up again, did he?" Terry asked as she came into the living room.

"No," she snapped. "A couple of drunks."

His face tensed. "Any trouble?"

"No. Make me a cuppa, will you?"

"What do you know then?" He asked her after putting the kettle on.

"Not much. Jim came in for a drink, that was about the high-light."

"How did he take the news?"

She pulled a face. "What news?"

"I saw Geoff as I was leaving. Reckons they've laid some staff off up there. Didn't Wendy say he worked on the factory floor?"

"Well, he never said anything. He seemed okay when he left. Bit agitated, but that's how he is. He said he couldn't sleep last night for that cat."

"Oh," he said, smiling. "You mean the crying infant." Behind him the kettle clicked.

"It's a cat." She smirked at him as he went into the kitchen. "For God's sake don't get him thinking it's anything else."

7

After the worst hangover he'd ever experienced in his life, Bundrick phoned work to see if anything had changed. It was only as he was putting the phone back down that he realised how much he'd been banking on good news. He managed to resist another drink until dusk by spending the day curled into a ball on the sofa. By the time it was dark he'd finished off the second bottle he'd had in his holdall.

The following day he phoned work again, but things were the same. That night, he made a start on Wendy and Graeme's drinks cabinet. The next morning, he felt so guilty that when his headache had subsided, he went to the off-licence and replaced everything he'd drunk, walking there and back, deciding that driving wasn't a good idea. Instead of going straight home Bundrick walked the streets for a while, the fresh air clearing his lungs and mind, the sound of the bottles chinking together in his bags oddly soothing. Feeling a bit more himself, he quickened his pace, ready to return home. But as he turned into the rows of terraces the image of 'The Ratcatcher's Inn' returned to him. Realising he wasn't quite ready to be cooped up again after all, he moved along the road away from the houses, heading instead for the church.

Walking along the circular path of flat gravestones, he looked at some of the more decrepit vertical ones; many looked as if they were about to faint, either propped up or weighed down by the moss that crowded in around them.

As he was making his way back to the entrance, an idea struck him: he'd been looking at everything the wrong way. Yes, the two things in life he did have which gave him security, his home and job, had both suddenly gone, but he'd hated both of them. If things changed, then he had to change with them. Not that he had any choice in the matter. But maybe that was a good thing. It all depended on his perspective; and there were always at least two interpretations to everything; he might not have a job anymore, but he didn't have to worry about money because he had savings. And he still had a roof over his head for the time being, and didn't have any rent to pay. And how long had it been since he'd had a holiday? Eight years? *Well*, he decided as he strode along the path of gravestones, *I'm having one now*.

As he was leaving the churchyard, an elderly man with a small bunch of flowers scowled when Bundrick smiled at him; when he heard the bottles knocking together, he looked away. *It doesn't necessarily mean he thinks I'm an alcoholic,* Bundrick thought, still smiling. Perspective. It was all about perspective.

As he let himself in through the back door, he thought he could hear the youths hammering again but ignored them. Putting the fresh bottles into the cabinet he went back to the kitchen, which already had become his favourite room. Making himself a strong black coffee, he sat down and put his feet up on another chair, inhaling the coffee and the silence.

From the living room he recognised the slight rattling sound of something being squeezed through the letterbox. Picking up the postcard of a grimacing Maori with a spear in his fist, he turned the card over and read:

Greetings from New Zealand! Hi Jim! Just arrived, safe and sound (four hours late though!). Weather about same as home. Company good (they're sat next to us in the pub!). Lovely and peaceful here, you'd love it! Luv, Wendy and Graeme. PS Will phone you soon.

Putting the card on the coffee table he wished he *was* with them, so much, in fact, it almost hurt.

Later, when Rebecca called, he was surprised to find he welcomed the company. In the kitchen she talked about their schooldays for longer than he felt comfortable with, only managing to change the subject by asking her if she wanted a coffee. Waiting for the kettle to boil, she asked what he'd been doing with himself. Instead of replying, he showed her the postcard.

"Sounds lovely," Rebecca said.

"I wish I was there with them," Bundrick said without thinking.

Rebecca looked concerned. "Oh?"

"No, I don't mean anything's wrong, I just...well, you know. Sounds idyllic."

"Certainly quieter. Mind you, it's been a lot better here since..." she screwed up her face. "You do know about what happened, don't you?"

Now he could find out the truth. Behind him, the kettle clicked off. "You mean next door?" he said, trying to sound calm as he made the coffee. "I heard something. Is it true, then?"

"Yes. It was terrible." She shook her head. "He just gave up. Locked himself in there. And the smell was..." she stopped, stared down at the table for a few seconds. "I used to go round every few days to see how he was. He didn't have anyone else." Taking the mug Bundrick held out to her, she nodded her thanks. "The smell came through the floor. If you look, there's a small space between his wall and the wall to the woodyard, and it gets filled up with all kinds of rubbish. A while before he died, I noticed that his living room wall was damp. When I turned up a bit of the carpet to look, the boards were black."

"Didn't he do anything about it?"

Taking a sip of her coffee, she shook her head. "He promised me he would. But after that I couldn't get him to let me in. He told me it was in hand and to leave him alone. I think his mind was going a bit, at the end. The last time I heard him through the letterbox his voice was-" she shrugged. "Well, it didn't sound like him. He normally had such a manly voice."

"Are you sure it wasn't a cat?" Bundrick asked. "I thought I heard one again last night."

"He didn't have a cat. And he never left the house or let anyone in besides me. Then he stopped answering the door altogether. At the inquest they made me feel like an idiot."

"Why?"

"Because," she said, smiling bitterly, "at the inquest they said I couldn't possibly have heard him that last time. You see, when they brought him out of there they had to carry him out in the chair he'd been sitting in, his body was so badly decomposed. Part of that was put down to the state of the room – the whole place was crawling with mould. But they said the body was so decayed he must have been dead for at least four weeks. But I heard him – or thought I did at the time – through the letterbox the week before they broke the door down."

For a while they both sat in silence. Eventually Rebecca laughed into her hand; Bundrick did his best to join in. "I shouldn't be laughing really, it terrified me at the time. But the noises stopped, they put a new concrete floor in and made the place habitable again. As you can see though, nobody wants it."

"Hardly surprising," he said quietly.

"But it shows how wise you can be after the fact. I know now those noises were just a cat, and they can't have come from inside his house. But the sound carries in a strange way around these old houses. Anyway, at least someone's bought that old woodyard for redevelopment. That might smarten things up a bit round here. I mean, all that rotten timber lying around, it can't be healthy. Anyway," her face suddenly burning, she rose awkwardly and banged into the table, the coffee in her mug threatening to spill over, "I'd better get back home now. Bye, then." Clumsily shutting the door after her, it bounced off her heel and sprung open again, sending a chill draught of air into the room.

8

God, what a tactless thing to say, Rebecca thought as she closed the gate. And why on Earth had she mentioned Moffatt? And after she'd warned Terry about mentioning the *child*!

He'd been reluctant to discuss their school days, too, she mused. They'd been a close little gang there, for a while. But that was over twenty years ago.She found herself feeling sorry for him, and figured she knew why Wendy had asked her to keep an eye on him; he was that kind of person. But he was also an adult and must be a lot more together than she gave him credit for; he hadn't even mentioned losing his job. Perhaps he already had something else lined up.

9

The next couple of days saw the last of the summer fade into full-blown autumn. Strong winds blew into the terrace, bringing with them the leaves from the few gnarled old trees that remained in the area. The rain lashed down, swirling old newspapers and mud and other rubbish along the cobblestones towards the woodyard wall. Bundrick spent much of this time crouched before the living room window with the raised net curtain resting on his head like a veil, pondering on past events, and what might be around the corner. The conversation he'd had with Rebecca seemed to *confirm* something to him, but what he wasn't sure what. He wasn't shocked by what she'd told him, just saddened. Maybe Moffatt was buried in the churchyard he'd been in earlier. When the weather cleared, he'd go and look; the old man would get at least one visitor.

Sitting in the kitchen the next day, he looked at the door in the right-hand wall and remembered the basement. Finding a small and badly stained key on the ring, he wrestled with the door until it opened.

Stepping into the darkness, something light brushed against his face. Grabbing at it, he pulled. After a long delay, a dim bulb in the ceiling below popped on, leaving him just enough light to get down the stairs, his footsteps like clopping horse's hooves on the boards. He was surprised to find the ground down there was earth; for some reason he'd expected stone. When he realised the ceiling was low enough even for him to touch it, he smiled.

Graham had told him they'd only been down a couple of times since moving in, mainly to store things until they decided what to do with them; their cardboard boxes, covered with brown tape, were wedged over in the left-hand corner of the room.

He stopped smiling long enough to let out a sigh of contentment. If old houses had a certain romance about them then their basements were the most romantic places of all, a dank, mysterious world tucked away below that few, sometimes even the owners of the house, seemed to care about.

From what he could make out, the basement covered the entire length of the house, although the piles of junk leaning against the walls distorted its size. The junk was fascinating: what he'd taken for a printing press turned out to be a rusty mangle; further down, a small collection of twisted brown tubes must've been discarded pipes. For a split second the overhead light dimmed before coming back on twice as bright as before. Over to the right the wall between the two houses looked oddly fragile; in the bright light the bricks resembled huge blocks of brown sugar sealed in with black icing. Water ran down the dark stones, dropping into a pool of mud below in a series of soft splashes.

Between the drops he heard something else, a noise like breath across the lip of a wine glass. As he concentrated on it it got louder, until it wasn't a breathy sound at all, but a low, keening whine.

Moving closer to the wall, Bundrick listened. The noise was coming from next door, he was certain. Surely the cat couldn't have got into Moffatt's basement? Maybe it was just the strange acoustics of the buildings that Rebecca had mentioned. But there was a rhythm to it, a pattern almost like language, full of sorrow, like overheard grief.

'Hello?' He called out.

His voice sounded ineffectual between the cold walls. But suddenly, the noise stopped. The bulb dimmed once more, not regaining its intensity when it blinked back a few seconds later. With a small shiver he went back up the steps, turned off the light and closed the door.

To take his mind off what had happened, he switched on the television. As the picture began to form a long, thin, leafless branch crept over the woodyard wall, banging itself against the side of Moffatt's house. The wind, he told himself.

Only the wind.

10

The following morning, Bundrick opened the curtains to find the rain had stopped. Putting on a jacket anyway, he locked the door behind him, and was half-way up the street when he remembered something.

Turning, he went back to the wall and peered into the gap. Seeing the great black mound of leaves and mud squashed into the small space reminded him of the wall in the basement. Perhaps the rot had gone down deeper than anybody suspected.

He went the long way round to the shops, determined not to be intimidated by an abandoned pub and a few sulky adolescents. He had to try and change. Nearing the wall and the clank of hammers once more, he used the words as a mantra. The legs on the wall were closer to him now, perhaps a foot nearer the ground. He glanced across at the youths but seeing the expressions on their faces he looked away again and hurried past; they weren't so much knocking the wall down as beating it down, both looking furious.

The crow was still there, he saw a little further on. Hadn't they thought to move it? But then he spotted another lying a few yards away, also with its claws pointing in the air. As before there were no obvious signs of attack. If the youth's expressions were anything to go by, he wouldn't have put it past either of them. But where was the blood?

Wanting to look again in the woodyard, he stopped a safe distance away, the hammering barely audible behind him. Standing on tiptoe, he peeped over a lower section of the wall.

Among the overgrown weeds and crushed beer cans, a couple of heavily stained mattresses and something resembling a fridge leaned against a half-hidden pile of rotting timber. From here, Bundrick had a clear view all the way to the terraces. Just behind the wall as it butted onto Moffatt's house were two stunted trees, stripped of bark. The nearest one was slightly bigger and darker, and looked like it was bending over the smaller one, its one long branch pointing in the wind.

How long he spent looking at them he wasn't sure; the clanking brought him back to his surroundings; they must really be hammering the wall hard if he could hear it from this distance. Walking away he tried to imagine what the woodyard would look like with houses growing out of it, rather than rotten trees and waterlogged timber. Nearing "The Ratcatcher's Inn" he wondered why nobody had turned it into houses.

Pausing for a second, he listened but heard nothing. Not that he had any desire to go back there; it was obviously unsafe. And he knew from bitter experience that places like that were best avoided. As he moved away, several large black birds shot through its exposed timbers as if fired from a cannon.

Standing in the queue at the supermarket he couldn't stop thinking about the youths and the crows. "A murder of crows", wasn't that the expression? But it was the youths that worried him the most; they'd looked so angry, pounding that wall.

Suddenly he felt warm. His forehead was damp, and his pulse started to quicken. He tried not to fidget, but suddenly wanted to get home quickly.

Remembering his earlier promise, he drew in a breath. What happened to not being frightened by a few teenagers? If he wanted to walk past them, he had every right. Why should they bother the likes of him? Going past them again would prove he was getting worked up about nothing. And if he still felt anxious afterwards, he could try that book on hypnotism.

To his relief, another till opened up. A few minutes later he was heading back in the direction of the ruined pub. After a deep breath he made himself slow down as he passed, staring at it as if daring it to make a noise. Leaving it behind him, Bundrick got the feeling that something had changed. Yes, the hammering had stopped, but that wasn't it; it wasn't something so obvious, so simple. It was just *different*. Perhaps they were having a break. Whatever it was, the feeling wouldn't go away.

As he was stepping over the first of the dead crows, he heard raised voices coming from the other side of the wall. He quickened his pace, but the voices became louder, more aggressive, the words muffled by the brick. A sudden shout close by made him jump, as did a second one; the youths must only be a matter of inches from him on the other side of the wall. A third exclamation was abruptly cut off, replaced by a sharp, swishing noise then a sickening thud, followed by several more, which he felt rather than heard.

When something landed heavily against the wall inches away from him he froze, paralysed by the nearness of the violence. There was a scream then the swishing sound again, but the blow must've missed because he felt the wall vibrate as he cowered against it.

"Get your hands off me!" a ragged voice yelled; a split second later the wall shook again.

The voice – or rather its ragged quality – shocked him into action. Racing along the street, the bottles in his bags chimed against each other. In the terrace, Rebecca was getting into her car. Seeing the expression on his face her smile changed to a look of alarm. As she started to speak, Bundrick shouted over her.

"Call the police, they're killing each other!" he pointed uselessly behind him. As he did a further scream was followed by another thud. "Hurry! *Please!*"

As Rebecca took her phone from her pocket, Bundrick noticed the bags he was carrying seemed heavier. Looking into them both were now full of broken glass; alcohol poured through the bags' air holes onto the cobbles.

"I'll – I'll just—" he said, looking round at Rebecca. But she was talking on the phone.

Standing by the kitchen door, he carefully lifted shards of broken glass from the carriers, putting it the bin. Seeing that one bottle remained intact, he unlocked the door and put it in the kitchen before going back outside.

Standing on the step, he tried to get his breath before going back to Rebecca. He'd just about managed it when he heard something to his right. There was only one place it could be coming from.

He walked as quietly as he could, afraid any sudden noises would stop it. Opening Moffatt's gate, the wood grated against the path with a noise that set his teeth on edge. When he finally got the gate closed, the noise, if anything, was louder. This close, he could make it out as a thin cry, a hollow rising and falling. He looked around quickly for a cat but knew he wouldn't see one – once you heard a noise like that you never forgot it. Standing in the empty garden he was back in another world, and he was helpless.

"No," he whispered as the crying seemed to fill his body, his shoulders shaking, "not again, please-"

"Jim? Are you alright?" Rebecca was only a few feet away and coming towards him. He looked at her, startled. *She'd been there that day too*, he remembered.

He had to say something; if he didn't, she'd only guess. "I lost my job," he told her, his eyes clouding over. "And *that*—" he pointed back to the wall, his finger shaking.

Opening Moffatt's gate, she led him from the garden, his head bowed. As they got to the road a police car pulled up next to the large hole in the wall further down.

Although he didn't sleep it wasn't until late evening that he came back to life. Staring down at the two-thirds empty whisky bottle on the table, he noticed a long, lightning-shaped crack running along the bottle, its tip seemed to point at him.

Outside, the wind had started to howl, and rain smashed against the windows. Apart from the faint orange blob of a streetlight hovering on the back wall, the room was in darkness. He looked again at the bottle: the only thing left from the afternoon's drama intact. He'd spent the hours since wanting to get drunk, but when he managed, albeit shakily, to stand up, he realised he couldn't even do that properly. Sitting back down, he slopped more amber liquid into his glass.

It felt odd that he'd been so affected by what'd happened, because at the time it almost felt like it was happening to someone else; when the police car had pulled up and he'd tried to explain what was going on he'd stumbled over his words, as though he was guilty of something himself.

"One of them shouted, 'Get your hands off me!'" he told the officer. "I couldn't make out the rest. But they were killing each other. I know they were."

What remained of the wall sprawled across the pavement, amongst the rubble two large black objects wobbled slightly in the wind. One of the officers spoke into his radio, asking where the ambulance was. The other, younger one looked like he was going to be sick. When Rebecca saw the state the teenagers were in she turned away. Bundrick had too, but the scene stayed in his head; raw, red faces plastered down with slicked red hair, the ripped clothing, the unmoving bodies surrounded by debris. Even the skip was covered in blood; several long, smeared fingerprints weaving across its yellow surface.

He had no memory of the ambulance arriving or taking them away; the bodies just seemed to vanish. The older of the officers thanked him for alerting them, then Rebecca took him home. Sitting him at the kitchen table, she phoned somebody to tell them she'd be late. After that it was a blank.

"Get your hands off me." The words kept repeating in his head until they were just noises, noises he was sure couldn't have heard from a teenager. Draining another glass, he listened to the rain

instead of the voice. Getting unsteadily to his feet he turned on the light, closed the curtains, and flopped back into his chair.

"There wasn't a cat next door," he said into the silence, his voice slurred. "And Rebecca said the noise stopped when Moffatt was taken away."

And it started again when he'd arrived. Then there was what happened at the wall; things like that don't happen without reason. They must be connected. And what about the crows? They were a sign of bad luck. "I've always been unlucky," he mumbled. "Must all be me, then."

Then he remembered something from that blank period: he'd asked Rebecca if she'd seen them.

"God, is that's what they were? There must have been a dozen in that skip." She'd said.

"But why? Why do you think that was?" He'd said nervously. "All in that same place next to the wall. Where they both went crazy." And wasn't there a hole there now too, next to the skip? There hadn't been one before.

His eyes started to droop, his chin knocking against his chest. He sensed something close to him but couldn't lift his head or open his eyes to see who it was.

You always look so worried, Wendy was saying. *You'll have the whole place to yourself. Relax.*

Yes, relax. There was a book he was going to look at, that would help –

There was a man in ripped clothes surrounded by a mob. When he staggered back against a tree a flock of large black birds flew from its branches, cawing. A woman stepped forward, kneeing him in the groin; as he rose slightly, a second man punched him in the stomach.

"Get your hands off me!" the man against the tree yelled.

For a second Bundrick's eyes clicked open. There was a book upstairs—

Despite the din a faint keening cry could be heard. At the edge of the mob, a face turned to see what it was.

"Get that child out of here!" they yelled.

It wasn't a cat; he knew it wasn't a cat…

Opening his eyes again, Bundrick looked around the room as if he'd never seen it before. There was a whisky bottle on the table next to him, a long crack running along its side.

He had to try and relax. Wendy had a book about hypnotism – perhaps that would help.

Stumbling upstairs to his room, he found the book straight away as if he'd been pulled to it. He started turning the pages but his eyes were closing again. He had to stay awake long enough to concentrate; the rain was drumming on the window, but it had to be something visual, something inside the room.

Eventually his half-closed eyes found the wardrobe door, but its horizontal white slats kept going out of focus. As he had down-stairs, he sensed there was something in the room with him, the feeling growing stronger as his eyes got heavier.

He tried once more to concentrate on the slats, but the room went black, and he felt himself falling forward onto the bed. As his head hit the mattress a small voice began talking, telling him things, asking him questions; he tried to escape the voice by press-ing his face into the duvet, but it kept getting louder, more in-sistent. Then, just before he blacked out the voice changed, be-came deeper, and he wondered why Wendy was calling him in the middle of the night.

#

The pattering of rain on the windows woke him the following afternoon, an endless torrent of tears cascading down the glass that upset him so much he had to look away. After washing, he collected the post that wasn't his from the mat in the living room. Phoning work, he asked Hargreaves if anything had changed. As the other man spoke Bundrick stared at the answer machine but didn't know why.

"You'd be as well looking for other work, I think, Jim," Hargreaves told him.

Hanging up, he was about to get some tablets for his headache when he realised what was bothering him about the answer machine. But according to the display nobody had called. Before he had a chance to think why that didn't make sense there was a knock at the kitchen door.

11

Despite spending half the night thinking about it, Rebecca still wasn't sure it was the best idea. Terry had gotten a call around eleven the night before; his older brother had been taken ill again. Despite the lateness of the hour, he'd had to go. But the timing wasn't great.

"He was in such a state, though, Terry," she'd told him. "I mean, it was horrible, but he shouldn't have reacted like that."

"So, what was he doing at Moffatt's?" he asked her.

"I don't know. He said he'd lost his job and I never got a chance to ask. It was like he was listening for something."

At that point the phone rang. She hadn't even mentioned the crows or the significance he seemed to place on them, or how he'd sat there in his kitchen in a kind of trance, mumbling that it was all his fault. Later on, she thought she'd heard him sobbing through the wall.

As the lights of Terry's car moved away from the windows, she decided to go to bed. Just as she'd been about to drop off, she thought heard a voice through the wall. For a brief second, she thought there were two, but put it down to the wind howling around the terrace.

Half an hour later she was still awake. Standing at the window, she looked out onto the woodyard. Perhaps the noise had come from there; it wouldn't have been the first time. And then she saw the thing that had kept her awake the rest of the night.

Scurrying through the clutter of the yard in some agitation Rebecca saw a small, child-like figure. She'd been about to open the window to call out to it when it occurred to her it could be Bundrick – he was little bigger than a child, after all. Whoever it was, they raced through the undergrowth as if looking for something. When she eventually lost sight of it, it was almost with a feeling of relief; the idea that it might've been her old school friend was too upsetting. That mumbled phrase "it all must be me, then" came back to her. Had losing his job affected him so much?

She managed to put off going round until it was nearly time for her afternoon shift in the pub. When he opened the door, she tried hard to keep the worry off her face. His skin was deathly pale beneath his stubble, and his hair was stuck up as if he'd been electrocuted. If he'd slept at all, it was in the clothes he was wearing, which were dirty and rumpled.

"How are you?" she asked, knowing the answer.

"Oh, fine. I've only just got up. Can I get you something to drink?"

She looked at her watch. "No, I can't stay. I just popped round to see if you were okay. Terry sends his regards. He said he saw you the other day."

"Right." He appeared to be thinking. "Have you heard anything about—" he pointed over his shoulder.

"No. The police are still there, though."

As Rebecca looked at him, he seemed to drift before her eyes. She couldn't ask him if he'd been at the woodyard while he was like this.

"Well, bye, then," she said. Looking back when he didn't close the door, she saw that he hadn't moved, the same vacant look still on his face.

12

"Yes, it was me. That heard them, I mean."

Bundrick had left the house with the feeling that something wasn't right, that something else wanted his attention. The trick, he knew, was not to think about it. A long walk would be just the thing.

"It's a good thing you did, too, Mr Bundrick," one of the officers said.

"Heard them, that is," the other interjected, shaking his head.

"Why?" His heart thudded hard. "Are they alright?"

"One of them isn't," the first officer told him. "He's still in a coma. We think he was the one that started it. The other one's not as badly injured, but he's not making a lot of sense."

As the officer was talking, a head popped out of the small tent next to the skip. Bundrick felt even guiltier. "What's the tent for?" he asked.

"Is there anything else you can tell us, perhaps something you forgot yesterday?" The first officer asked, ignoring his question.

"Well, I went past the wall earlier and they both seemed angry – like they were taking it out on the wall. And there were the crows on the floor. Rebecca – that's Mrs. Wallace – said she saw about a dozen more in the skip." He felt stupid saying these things, but noticed the head from inside the tent was still listening.

"Well, I'd better go." Bundrick said when they didn't respond. As he walked away, he half expected them to call him back, the way they did in police shows. Why hadn't they answered him when he'd asked about the tent?

Passing the "The Ratcatcher's Inn" he felt nauseous; he wasn't just anxious now but downright afraid, though he didn't know why. Recalling his promise to change, he made himself stop and look at it again, breathing in large gulps of air as he did so.

"Ugly, isn't it? They should knock it down, don't you think?"

Startled, he turned to see a man of about seventy standing beside him.

"What happened to it, do you know?" Bundrick asked eagerly.

"Oh, it burnt down years ago and nobody took it back over." After sucking on his cigarette and putting his plastic bag on the ground, he continued. "Whole area's gone to pot. This place is the same," he glanced back over his shoulder. Bundrick assumed he meant the two youths. "I worked in that yard for over twenty years from when it opened. Now they're going to build cheap flats on it. Why can't they leave things be?"

Bundrick asked him if he'd heard what'd happened. As he told him the old man remained impassive. "The skip was full of dead crows as well," Bundrick added.

To his surprise the old man nodded. "They probably flew into the wall. Seen it happen a few times over the years. Still, it'll stop the kids hanging around, I suppose."

Bundrick wasn't sure he'd heard correctly. "The crows fly into the wall?"

"Aye. Don't know why like, but there you go." The old man took another drag on his cigarette. "Aye, twenty years in that yard. Falling orders, that's why it shut, you know."

If he could've got a word in, he'd have told the old man he knew how that felt. Everything seemed to be a coincidence lately. Or maybe nothing was … But the man was talking again.

"Mind you, the ground was dodgy in that yard, always was. You can see it in those trees over there."

Suddenly he felt the need to get away. Giving a hurried good-bye, Bundrick headed for the terrace.

Despite an effort to avoid it, he walked over to the wall and looked into the gap. It took him a while to make it out, but he was sure there'd been a change; the mud and leaves stuck in there were sloping up against the side of the house, perhaps three or four feet high, and had taken on a sinister aspect, like the trees in the woodyard. The idea was ridiculous, he knew. But when he went back inside, he couldn't stop thinking about the mulch sucking at the brickwork next door, weakening the stone, oozing through the walls.

Making coffee, he realised he wasn't any closer to remembering whatever it was he thought he'd forgotten. But it was becoming increasingly hard to concentrate on anything at the moment the way things were going.

Perhaps it would help if he went a bit further out. He'd heard somewhere that the park a few miles away was full of sculptures by a local artist. It wasn't really his thing, but it was an excuse to get away for a while.

Not having driven since he'd arrived at the Masons, it took him a while to find his car keys. Out on the road, he noticed the engine was noisier than usual. Glancing in his rear-view mirror, he saw the road rapidly diminishing behind him. When he realised what he was doing, he eased his foot off the accelerator.

The park appeared to be empty as he drove into it, the two cars in the parking area sitting in opposing corners like sworn enemies. Apart from an unseen man calling out for a dog, the only sound was his footsteps across the thin layer of gravel to the grass. Spots of rain dotted the air and turned everything grey. Beneath the branches of trees, he kicked horse chestnuts into the undergrowth.

Following the path that wound between the trees, he was surprised to see one in the middle of the path. Even so, he couldn't understand his apprehension when only a few feet away he realised it wasn't a tree at all, but one of the sculptures.

Despite being a twisted lump of rusting metal, the sculpture looked like it was in agony. Corkscrewing its way out of the ground to a height of about four feet, its thin, tapering, finger-like branches pointed further into the park towards other bits of metal, apparently variations on the theme. Without stopping to look at the inscriptions he kept going, past what appeared to be fenceposts nailed to a section of wall to a café near an exit. Inside, and glad to be out of the drizzle, he took a pot of tea to a seat in the corner and looked at the old photographs on the wall opposite. Beneath them, a glass case was full of rumpled yellow pages.

As he waited for his tea to cool his gaze kept returning to the case. Leaving his table, he went over to it. The papers were filled with drawings, preliminary sketches for the sculptures. A small, printed card taped to the edge of the glass was completely covered in neat, blocky handwriting. But the word "Moffatt" he was sure was bigger than the rest. He stared at it, convinced it was an hallucination.

But what about the sculptures? They looked just like—

It couldn't be the same man. Getting one of the leaflets from the counter, he saw the name again. Looking back at the glass case, he read: "*Sketches provided by Matthew Moffatt from his own collection, for the—*"

"Excuse me," Bundrick asked the man in green overalls behind the counter, "Matthew Moffatt – is he still alive?"

The man shook his head. "He died a few months ago. I take it you've seen his work, in the park?"

"Yes. It's…" He wanted to speak but didn't know what he could say.

"Tortured, I think is the word you're looking for. He was—"

"Do you know anything about him?" he cut in. "About his life?"

"It's all in the leaflet," the man said, looking at the card in Bundrick's hand. "He had a lot of tragedy in his life though, with his daughter and everything."

Bundrick froze. "His daughter?"

"Hmm. She disappeared, her and several other children around the same time, but they never found her. They think she was abducted – it's not a new thing, you know. But she seems to have been the last one – at least no others were reported after her. It's all in the leaflet though, as I say… are you alright, sir?"

Mechanically, Bundrick turned from the counter and walked back out into the rain, not noticing how heavy it had become.

He only found his car so quickly because it was the only one still left in the car park. Slumping into the driver's seat, he looked at the crumpled leaflet in his hand. Seeing the words *"Mea Culpa" by Matthew Moffatt* printed at the top his stomach spasmed. Visions of the trees in the woodyard came back to him, the smaller one in particular. Mea culpa – *my guilt.*

What was he living next door to? For a second an image he had no recollection of flared in his head, a man standing against a tree. This was followed by a vivid memory – being stuck behind Rebecca's car when he first arrived at the Masons' house, the registration plate reflecting back at him in the glare of his headlights. The first three letters: MEA.

Of course, she knew what'd happened to him! Had she told Graeme and Wendy as well?

Mea Culpa.

Without success he tried to reason it through, but every time he did the thoughts slid away from him. Giving it up, he gunned the engine and sped out of the car park, slamming on the brakes outside the church. He had to make sure.

Almost immediately he found Moffatt's stone, although he was sure he hadn't spotted it last time. As the rain ran into his eyes, he checked the dates and the name: It was the same man. His wife's name was there as well, dead almost twenty years. But there was no mention of a daughter. Staggering backwards onto the path he noticed something else; of that whole row of headstones, Moffatt's was by far the shabbiest, its grey stone was duller and scruffier, and looked much older than a twenty year old stone should look. *Even his headstone*, Bundrick thought, going back to the car.

Driving back into the terrace his gaze locked on Rebecca's car, its registration plate as big as a billboard. Screwing up his eyes to blank it out, he only opened them in time to slam the brakes on and avoid crashing into the wall.

He had to talk to her. Knocking on her door, he got no response. She might be at the pub; and even if she wasn't it seemed a good place to go.

The traffic lights took an eternity to change. The pub on the other side of them looked miles away. When he heard beeping noises, he had to think what they were: the lights had turned green. He ran towards the pub.

Just as he was about to enter, he heard raucous laughter and voices. Rather than push his way past, he waited for them to come out. But the voices didn't seem to get any closer. Looking impatiently towards the black maw of the entrance, he felt a draught on his face, and tensed; above him, the huge skeletal timbers of "The Ratcatcher's Inn" hovered in the air like rotted propellers.

A sudden blast of music from the real pub brought him back. Pushing through the door, a man and a woman standing just over the threshold grudgingly moved aside to let him in.

He looked up and down the length of the bar but couldn't see Rebecca. A barmaid asked him if he wanted a drink. Ordering a double scotch, he knocked it back before he handed over the money. After a couple more he sat down, bothered by the barmaid's expression. Taking the sculpture park leaflet from his pocket, he read it again.

When Bundrick went back to the bar Rebecca was at the far end. Shouting much louder than he'd intended, several people turned round but he forgot about them as she made her way over.

"Jim?" she asked quizzically.

"I've just been to the park," he told her, handing her his glass and a fistful of change. "Matthew Moffatt – he was a sculptor!" He stared at her hard, to see if her expression gave anything away.

She gave him a strange look. "Yes, I know. I told you."

He felt like he'd been slapped. "When?"

"A couple of days ago. You asked if there was anything to do locally and I told you about the sculptures in the park."

Walking away from him, she went to get his drink.

"And I found out about the crows," he called after her.

"What about them?" She said over her shoulder.

"They fly into the wall because they *have to!*"

As it had outside, the pub seemed to dissolve around him.

They fly into the wall because they have to.

It made sense – that's where the workmen had been too, when they'd attacked each other. There was something about that spot – and now the police knew about it; that's why they had a tent there. And Moffatt had known about it and was somehow involved in it.

As if a switch had been flicked the pub appeared again, all light and noise, and he couldn't think straight. Turning, he saw Rebecca staring at him. Before she had a chance to speak, he left.

Outside, it was a shock to find the street in darkness. Rain bounced off the pavements, the drops lit from inside by the headlamps of passing cars. Running across both lanes of traffic, he fended off speeding cars with outstretched hands. He hurried into the terrace as fast as he could, but the cobbles were slippery with rain.

Despite the deluge Bundrick could see the last two houses had gone.

His senses deserted him as they had at the pub. Forcing himself to look along the rest of the row, all the other houses were there, ending with Rebecca's; after it there was nothing but blackness. Even the wall had gone; only the two trees remained, stunted and ugly in the poisoned earth.

He staggered forward slowly, his hands flapping out ahead of him. He didn't want to pass Rebecca's car and face the nothing ahead, but he kept going anyway. His hand knocked against something cold, something that shouldn't be there; after a moment of blind panic, he touched it again. Despite not being able to see it he knew it must be his car, because that was where he'd parked it earlier. He ran his hands across the invisible cold metal again, until its smoothness was replaced with a grittiness he knew must be the rust spot above the passenger door.

Moving away from the car, he looked at the emptiness ahead and tried to judge where the house was. Shuffling forward, he banged against the invisible brickwork of the wall, unlatching the gate, his fingers desperately searching for the door. When his fingers finally touched the wood, he let out a small cry; lower down, he found the door handle. His hands trembling, he got the key from his pocket and gripped it tight, terrified he might drop it. It took several attempts to find the keyhole; when he did the click of the lock sounded louder than it should, but he didn't care. Pushing at the door with all his weight, he fell inside. From the floor he kicked the door shut behind him, whimpering.

Despite the lack of light, the room was full of colour and shape. Crawling through the kitchen to the living room, he climbed onto the sofa, burying his face and upper body in cushions while his legs dangled over the edge. But he kept going, as if burrowing into the fabric of the sofa, then into sleep itself, only stopping momentarily to listen to the rumbling and crashing sounds around him. But almost immediately he was burrowing again, ploughing through the thick and heavy darkness that surrounded him.

13

Hearing more banging, Bundrick thought it must be the same noise he'd heard a few minutes earlier. Lifting himself from the cushions, his face prickled with heat. Narrowing his eyes against the bright glare of sunlight streaming through the windows, the clock on the mantelpiece said it was eight thirty. When the banging noise started again, he was sure it wasn't the same as the one he'd heard the night before. That had been a great thudding sound; this was just an agitated knocking.

Getting off the sofa, his limbs ached. Looking at himself in the hall mirror, he saw his hands and face were covered in dents and scratches. He was trying to remember the dream he'd had when the banging started again. It was coming from the kitchen.

It was a relief to see the back door locked and no silhouette in the glass. Why did Graeme have a *glass* door, anyway? This was a rough area, anybody could get in. He was still pondering it when he heard it again. A faint wisp of an idea from the night floated across his mind, but he dismissed it: there were no such things as ghosts. If anybody was there, he'd be able to see them. He shivered, but that was because the room was so cold. He needed coffee. Before he reached the kettle, he heard it again. Turning to his right, he watched as the cellar door vibrated in its frame.

He couldn't understand why it was so cold; the door was locked, so was the kitchen window. Maybe it wasn't that cold at all, maybe he was just uptight. The best thing he could do was empty his mind. As soon as he tried, his head filled with words.

I've been trying to tell myself all along. I'm still –

No, he couldn't believe that. But what about the empty space where the houses should have been last night, and all the other things that had been happening? But how could something like that be possible? He'd only looked at it for a few minutes.

Charging up the stairs, he searched frantically for the book on hypnotism. Had he really been in a trance all that time, since looking at the book? As he moved things around, he couldn't believe it was so easy to hypnotise yourself. But it explained how he'd forgotten Rebecca telling him Moffatt was a sculptor, and her strange looks.

The kitchen. It's still in the kitchen.

He found it on one of the chairs. Flipping through the pages, he remembered he'd been drinking that night too – no wonder he'd gone in so deep. Finding the right page, it said that getting out of a trance was just a matter of counting backwards.

Behind him the basement door rattled in its frame again. Telling himself it was part of the trance too, he ignored it.

"Five," he mumbled.

"For God's sake get that child away from here!" Someone yelled again above the din of the crowd, the cry of the infant.

Ignore it. "Four."

Hearing the voice, the child, a girl with long hair, stopped crying. As she did, she saw a man break free from the crowd and start towards her. More frightened than before, she ran as fast as she could past the houses, knocking on the doors of each one, trying to get away, so afraid

*that she barely knew what she was doing, barely noticed when none
of them opened.*

Behind him, the door rattled against its hinges.

"Three."

*Seemingly out of nowhere, rough hands grabbed her, pulling her
back along the street. "Back in the house," the man told her above her
panicked screams. "Just for a little while—"*

"Two."

*She tried to escape but the man held firm. Dragging her back to
the end house, he kicked the door open with his foot, by now half-
carrying her through the living room and into the kitchen, opening
the basement door with one hand as the girl struggled in the other.
"It's for your own good," he told her as he pushed her through the door,
"until we've taught him a lesson!"*

"One."

As Bundrick's eyes flew open, so did the cellar door behind
him, crashing against the wall, knocking a mop to the floor. An
icy blast of wind from below lifted the hair from his head and
shook the kitchen door, rattling is frame.

Slowly, he made his way to the basement door and reached
inside for the cord. The faint humming glow of the light was all
he could hear and feel as he walked down the steps, as if walking
into a dream, the draught pinching at his sleeves.

At the bottom he stopped, seeing something that didn't make
sense. He walked towards it slowly across the earth floor. A huge
opening had appeared in the wall separating the two houses, the
scattered piles of rubble laying on the ground reminding him of
the wall at the woodyard. The noises he'd heard in the night. But
how had it happened?

It didn't matter; it was enough that it had. Something – *somebody* – was trying to contact him and he thought he knew who it was. The same giddy excitement he'd felt outside the abandoned pub tingled in him as he rushed back up the stairs to get a torch. Finding one under the sink, he went back down.

As he approached the wall, a dank, cloying odour filled his nostrils. Shining the torch into the dark corner, something resembling discoloured foam clung to the strewn brickwork. Playing the beam across the intact section of the wall, he recognised it as fungus.

Dropping to his knees, Bundrick crawled through the hole into Moffatt's basement as the torch light bobbed across the debris. Getting to his feet on the other side, his breath caught in his throat.

The light played across a stack of old newspapers on the floor, liquefying amongst the muck sliding down the brickwork. As he picked up a handful, he let out a disgusted noise as the sodden lump started to tear in his hand, slopping back down onto the pile.

Otherwise, the basement was empty, the glare from the torch illuminating nothing but the honeycomb of bricks surrounding him until finally lighting up the small staircase to the right. He took the wooden steps carefully, wary in case the condition of the cellar had weakened them.

It never occurred to him that the door leading to the kitchen might be locked, and he didn't have the room to shoulder it open. He tried falling against it but it remained solid. Putting his back to the door, he raised his foot and kicked at it like a horse; after a few goes it started to give. As he kicked harder, the noise boomed in his ears; it was a good thing this was the end house, and nobody was in the Wallace's. Finally, the door burst open with a loud crack.

Stepping into the kitchen, the grey light outside was made greyer by the grease on the windows, making him feel like he was underwater. Turning off the torch, he looked at a gutted version of the kitchen he loved next door. It looked bigger because of the lack of furniture, and the once black-and-white floor tiles were now a washed-out black and grey. Moving across the floor, his feet felt cold and clammy through his socks.

In the hall the floor was bare, and the concrete looked darker than he felt it should; the skirting board was covered with a line of silt. Fine particles of moisture hung in the air, reminding him of his visit to the park – yet another link with Moffatt. Faded damp paper bubbled on the walls, only slightly darker where old picture frames had once hung. Hadn't Rebecca told him it'd all been cleaned up after Moffatt was removed?

On seeing the living room however, Bundrick began to question if she'd said that at all. The bare concrete floor was discoloured right up to the far wall. Here, large patches of creamy brown fungus spewed through cracks and holes in the wall and floor; plaster was scattered everywhere. In the corners, rotted clumps poked through the saturated wall and skirting board; large drops of moisture dripped onto the fungus like tears. Watching the drops, he was sure he could see the fungus growing. Grabbing a chunk from the wall it ripped apart like wet polystyrene, oozing water onto the floor like a squeezed sponge. He thought again about Moffatt, slumped in his chair as the room got damper, with the fungus sprouting around him, spreading as he decayed amongst it, and all the while that horrible keening whine ringing in his ears.

He checked the upstairs rooms to see if they were the same, but they were relatively clean, empty. Coming out of one of the bedrooms he thought he could hear a distant rapping sound; it took him a few seconds to realise it must be someone at his back door. Thundering down the stairs and through the kitchen, he opened the door to the basement and stepped inside. Closing the door behind him he started forward carefully, so not to slip on the weakened wooden steps.

But there was a push in the darkness, and the steps splintered and groaned as something tumbled down them. "Be quiet, child!" the man shouted as the door slammed shut. "It'll only be for a little while-"

Blinking the image from his mind Bundrick looked around and saw he was standing at the bottom of the steps, his arms rippling with cold. He was sure he hadn't fallen; but he was also sure he hadn't walked down the steps.

The knocking was louder now, impatient. His eyes adjusting to the dark, he crawled back through the hole in the wall, scrabbled to his feet and groped up the stairs. Upon entering the kitchen, he saw Rebecca's outline against the glass door.

14

As the door closed behind her, Rebecca let out a grunt of frustration.

"What's wrong?" Terry asked.

"I've just been talking to Mr. Warwick," she told him. "Last night when Jim left the pub…well, I told you what he was like. I'd only mentioned Moffatt's sculptures a day or two before—"

"Lapse of memory, that's all. Have them myself."

"No, there's more to it than that."

"What about Warwick?"

"He said he saw Jim last night, walking along the terrace. He was groping at the cars and the walls of the houses like he was blind." She didn't have to remind him of the banging noises they'd heard in the night.

"Look Reb, the man has just lost his job and he's a bit on edge, that's all. You said so yourself. He'd had a few drinks and was slightly the worse for wear."

"Mr. Warwick also said they've found bones near that wall they were knocking down. They think they're human."

Terry frowned at her. "What's that got to do with anything?"

She shrugged. "I don't know. I really don't know."

"You never told me what was wrong with Jim before."

She looked at him carefully. "Do you have time?"

"Think so."

"Wow," he said when she'd finished. "Maybe you should go round and see how he is, after all. Do you want me to go with you?"

"No, I'll be okay. Besides, you'll be late for work."

After giving her husband a distracted peck on the cheek, she tried to think of what she was going to say.

#

After five minutes of getting nowhere Rebecca decided the best thing was to just knock on his door and ask how he was. As she did, she thought back at how together he was when he'd arrived. Well, relatively so. Not unless he was just good at covering up his feelings; and it'd be hard to forget what happened when he was younger. She decided not to mention the bones they'd found. Rapping the glass again, she looked up and down the quiet, empty street, the only sound the blowing of the wind around the old houses. Seeing nothing in the glass door, she knocked again.

And why did he keep going on about those crows? They seemed really important to him. A strong gust seemed to come from nowhere; as it moved through the terrace it reminded her of a voice.

Now she was being ridiculous. Annoyed with herself, she knocked even louder, deciding that if he didn't come this time she was going back home. A sudden thundering noise close by made her jump.

There was no point standing around here spooking herself. About to turn away, she was startled when the door swung inward and Bundrick appeared in its place.

"Yes?" he said, gulping in air.

She tried her best not to look him up and down but couldn't help herself. He looked worse than before; his clothes were covered in dirt, and he wasn't wearing any shoes; his socks were caked in muck, as if he'd been walking across open fields; he even had streaks of earth on his face. As she watched he wiped at one furiously with his sleeve.

"Oh, hi. You seemed a bit worse for wear last night, so I..." at a loss for words, she said the first thing she could think of. "I got a postcard from Graeme and Wendy this morning. They seem to be enjoying themselves." She tried to smile but failed.

"Something's wrong, isn't it?" he asked, his voice shaking.

"Oh no, no," Rebecca said, shaking her head vigorously. "Nothing's—"

"What is it?" his voice was almost a shriek.

"Jim, I don't know whether it's a good idea to..." her words trailed off.

"You can't leave it like that!" he yelled, his voice unnaturally high. Embarrassed by his intense gaze, she looked past him into the kitchen. She wasn't sure why, but a chill went through her. She found she couldn't stop herself. "I've just been told – they found human remains in the woodyard. Near the wall."

Not for the first time it was as if she wasn't there. Bundrick's lips quivered, as if he was working something out. His face paled beneath the muddy patches.

"Jim," she said eventually, "please, tell me what's wrong."

"I know who they belong to," he said, coming back to her as the wind rose again. "I don't know his name, but they all killed him, and kept quiet about it. But Moffatt wasn't there when it

61

happened; he was with his daughter, trying to keep her quiet. They must've all known about that as well." He added softly, his voice barely carrying above the wind. "They were trying to protect the children, you see. And that's why her name isn't on the headstone."

Mumbling to himself he went back inside into the living room. Following him, she watched as he picked a leaflet off the coffee table, reading it as he paced around the small room.

She was about to speak when a dull thump nearby startled her. Rushing

past her, Bundrick went back into the kitchen; she got there in time to see him slamming the basement door, still mumbling.

She couldn't bear it any longer. Without saying goodbye, she headed for the door, only the open book on the kitchen table caught her eye. She recognised it immediately; one night when they'd been here Wendy had showed it to her. But it had been spotless then; now it was covered in fingerprints, most of which were around a paragraph at the top of the left-hand page ...*auto-suggestion, simply put, is a process whereby the individual unconsciously supplies the means for influencing their own behaviour or beliefs. Similarly –*

"Mea Culpa," Bundrick's voice behind her made her jump. "It means 'my guilt', Rebecca. It explains everything."

"Jim, I've got to go. Bye." Gripping the door handle tightly, she yanked it forward and walked out.

#

Pacing her kitchen floor a few minutes later Rebecca forced herself to stop, conscious of the fact she was imitating Bundrick. Eventually she made a decision.

Getting the address book from beside the window, she looked up a number she never thought she'd have to use. After an eternity an elderly man said hello.

"Er, hello," she said. "Could I speak to Graeme or Wendy, please?"

15

"They killed him and buried his body next to the wall. If what the old man said was true, it wasn't a woodyard then," Bundrick said, looking at the basement door. "It was a different area then, a different time – people stuck together in those days, kept things to themselves; nobody else need know. Only they didn't kill him, not really – he's the one making crows fly into the wall, and those two lads attack each other; he's even poisoned the woodyard and the trees. And I think that's why she hadn't wanted Moffatt to leave her because she thought she was next. He's getting stronger all the time. And closer – he's already managed to get into Moffatt's house once. And now they've disturbed him… And she was down there, alone, and needed someone; she can sense what I've been through with Rachel. You see, it wasn't Moffatt I had the close connection to at all – it was his daughter."

He turned to look at Rebecca, but she wasn't there. He hadn't even heard her leave. The last thing he remembered was seeing her looking at the book on the table. Her hands must have been filthy because the book was covered in fingerprints. Looking at the page he read the passage she must've read, but it made no sense to him. But that was probably a trick; he remembered what the book had done to him earlier.

Carrying it to the sink, he dropped it in. Taking a box of matches from the drawer, he lit one and touched the flame to the edge of the grubby page, watching it burn until a wisp of smoke like a long, accusing finger curled up at him.

Leaving it to burn in the sink, Bundrick went back to the cellar. Crawling back through the hole, he looked at the pile of rotting papers against the wall and felt certain this where she'd fallen when Moffatt locked her in. When he'd come back after dealing with the man, he must've realised what'd happened, and the questions that would be asked. But if he buried her where she fell, her disappearance could be attributed to the child killer.

Dropping to his hands and knees, Bundrick knew he could free her. He started to remove the papers, throwing slippery chunks behind him. It was only when he'd done it five or six times that he saw the date on one of the papers and an idea came to him. Carefully lifting the sodden edge of the next paper in the pile, he saw that the paper was from the previous year but had the same date. Below it, the next paper was the same. Quickly removing the others in the pile, he stopped at the last one; it was several years earlier than the others but again had the same date. Shining the light across the wet newsprint he could just make out the headline:

TWELVE MONTHS ON, STILL NO SIGN OF MISSING GIRL

Was this how Moffatt marked her death, a permanent reminder to himself of what he'd done, watching the pile of papers growing every year along with his guilt?

Moving the final paper away, Bundrick looked at the flat, damp earth in front of him. Scooping fistfuls of damp soil from the ground, it squirted through his fingers; black water ran down his shirtsleeves. Soon he was up to his elbows in it, a mushy black pool filled with treacly earth.

He was just starting to wonder how deep Moffatt had buried her when he saw something pale and solid jutting up from the hole. Then, through the sound of his ragged breathing he heard the familiar keening noise all around him.

"You don't have to stay here anymore," he shouted above it. "You can go to your family."

The crying got louder, piercing in his head.

"You feel responsible for what happened to that man, don't you? But that's silly. He was a bad man. He did bad things. It wasn't your fault." People had said similar things to him over the years; she didn't seem to believe it any more than he had, because the crying got louder.

Slowly, he bent to touch the bone in the soil. "And what happened to you was an accident," he said. "Your father didn't want you seeing what they were doing so he locked you in here. But you slipped."

An ice-cold blast of air blew through the basement. A few feet away, standing next to the stairs, a small girl with a milky-white face looked at him through the black hair hanging from both sides of her face. He felt a chill greater than the one that'd just gone through the basement when he saw how similar the girl was to Rachel.

"You can go now," Bundrick said eventually, his freezing breath misting her image.

Raising himself from the floor, he held out his hand to her and took a step forward, his eyes never leaving the girl's. When he was near enough to take her hand, she backed away from him until she was up against the wall, but she didn't stop; she melted through it, until all he could see was his own freezing breath in front of him.

For a second, he was stunned. It was obvious where she was going – but why? To finish what had been started? Or was it just childhood curiosity, the way it'd been with Rachel on the building site? But he knew he had to go after her. Scrambling back through the wall, he grazed his ankles and elbows in his rush to get upstairs and out to the woodyard.

It was raining, like it had been that day. Only now it was dark. Splashing through the puddles, he ran for the hole where they'd found the remains, relieved that the only thing stopping him reaching it was a piece of police tape. But there wasn't a hole there anymore, just a pool of dark water. And as he looked, he saw it wasn't water at all; it was too thick, almost as thick as the stuff he'd dug out of the girl's grave. It was only when it started bubbling that Bundrick knew it was blood.

As he watched it in horrified fascination, he sensed the girl standing at his side. The blood in the hole began to spit furiously, the bubbles erupting one after another as the liquid continued to boil. Finally, it spilled over the lip of the hole, running past him. He tried to call out to the girl, but she'd already gone, the blood running under her feet in a thick carpet, pink in the moonlight. It wasn't until the girl was nearly back at the woodyard wall that he saw that it wasn't blood any more, if it ever had been; it was a plank, like the one which had taken Rachel's life; and it wasn't Moffatt's house she was running towards, but one which was only half-built. Finally, Bundrick found his voice, but it was too late, because Rachel was at the end of the plank and it gave way and she screamed, and the shrillness of that scream was piercing the inside of his head before he had a chance to clamp his hands to his ears.

Lifting his face from the freezing mud, the sight of the walls confused him. Bundrick was still in the Wallace's basement. Above he could hear loud voices muffled by the brickwork.

Disoriented, he headed for the steps, sure he could hear a ringing noise coming from the kitchen. It was cut off before he reached the kitchen and replaced by a female voice he was sure he recognised. Hurrying up the final few steps, Bundrick pushed open the door to the kitchen, which was full of noise despite being empty.

"...please, if you're there pick up... Rebecca was worried about you, Jim...he's not answering, Graeme."

Then a male voice spoke. "Jim? He must be out. I don't know... I don't see what else we can do over here."

The woman's voice returned. "Jim? It's Wendy again. I'm going to contact Rebecca and get her to pop in on you...please look after yourself. Why didn't you tell us about your sister? All these years we've known you and you never even mentioned her—"

It wasn't until he heard the beep of the answer machine that he knew for certain he'd been listening to the phone. Now it had stopped he could hear the noises he'd noticed downstairs – loud, panicked voices, just like the day he'd lost Rachel, coming from outside.

As if still in a dream, he went through the house and opened the front door. Outside, the street was full of people wearing pyjamas, all huddled together in little knots. Seeing a small child clinging to its mother's legs, a lump came to his throat. Stepping into the street nobody noticed him, as if he were a ghost. He looked at the startled faces of the people standing there. The air heavy with shock and disbelief. Was this what it had been like for everyone else at the building site?

"I know what I saw," an elderly woman said to the small man next to her. "And you heard what she said behind us."

"But it doesn't make sense," the man, who looked as frail as the woman said as she played with her dressing gown. "These houses are solid, woman. Nothing can get through those walls, let alone through one and then through another."

"Then what's everybody doing out here?" she snapped. "The same thing's happened to all of us. You heard what-"

"I don't know, do I?" the old man snapped back. "But whatever it was, it can't have been that."

"I did it," Bundrick said quietly. "I released her. I set her free."

But they didn't hear him. "It's not even as if there's a girl round here looks like that. You've got too much imagination, that's your trouble."

After a while, people began going back indoors. A few at first, then the rest, a ripple of nervous laughter running through them.

"Probably someone's idea of a joke," the old man told his wife.

"Well," she snorted, following him back inside, "if that's what it was it wasn't in very good taste." A door slammed behind him. Then he was alone.

Looking at the night sky, he hoped she was at peace, not reliving that moment over and over again, looking for the sense of it. If she was at peace, then maybe he had a chance after all. Without looking back, he left the terrace, walking towards the building ahead silhouetted in the moonlight. As he got close to it, he

69

thought how peculiar it was, how half-built and half-ruined buildings could look so similar.

Pushing open its door as quietly as he could, he stepped inside.

16

Getting home from Terry's brother's the following lunchtime after a difficult night, the street was quiet. Seeing the red light on the answering machine, Terry groaned.

"Ignore it," he told her, as she walked towards the phone, "let's just go to bed."

They listened in silence as Wendy spoke.

"I have to go round and check," Rebecca said.

The door to the Mason's house was open. Reluctantly, she poked her head into the living room. "Hello?" There was no reply.

Then she smelled the burning. Finding the charred book in the sink, she went with increasing urgency through the rooms. She found nothing but an unmade bed upstairs and four holdalls full of Bundrick's belongings. Hearing a noise in the kitchen, she went downstairs.

It was freezing. To her right, the door leading to the basement was wide open; cold air blew up from below. Tugging on the cord at the top of the stairs, she went down.

As she did, she thought her eyes were playing tricks on her. The floor was strewn with brick and mortar, and there was a hole in the wall between the houses almost big enough for a child to walk through.

"Jim?" she called out. "Jim, it's Rebecca."

With a sick feeling she realised what the situation reminded her of. There'd been about a dozen of them that day, playing hide and seek among the half-built houses. She hadn't seen it happen, but she remembered Rachel – she'd been a few years younger than the rest of them, and Jim had been looking after her for the day. She could see Jim in her mind, running forward and screaming, scrabbling away the rubble to get to her, yelling that it was his fault. And later, when the ambulance came and took her away and nobody knew where he was. When the police found him, they had to pull him out of a tiny space beneath the floors. He wouldn't stop crying, refused to leave.

"Jim?" she called out again as another gust of wind came through the gap at her, toppling a brick from the ruined wall.

Looking at the rubble, she wondered about those thumping noises in the night: was he responsible? But there was so much rubble on this side of the wall as well that he must've been through more than once and kicked some of it back through on his way out.

Back in the kitchen she found Terry looking for her.

"He's gone," she said. "We'll have to go look for him."

They got as far as the end of the road, where a small group of people were milling around outside the abandoned pub.

"It's like last night, this," someone in the group said.

"Why what happened last night?" someone else asked.

But Rebecca didn't hear the answer; instead, a block of ice dropped in her stomach as she remembered Terry saying he'd seen Jim outside the pub a few days earlier. She was just about to ask what was going on when an old man told her.

"There's someone stuck inside," he said, sucking on his cigarette. "Part of the floor's caved in. What? Don't know, love. Could be an adult or a kiddie, listening to them crying. We've called an ambulance. There – you can just hear it. Listen."

At first, she couldn't hear anything. Then, through the chatter of the crowd she was just able to make out a thin, keening whine coming from inside the derelict building, mercifully drowned out moments later by the answering cry of the ambulance. But instinctively Rebecca knew it was already too late; it would be the thin, keening whine which would fill the silence for a long time to come.

You, Not Running into Me

A Short Story

The first time it happened it was the coat I spotted first, a coat I hadn't seen anyone else wearing in years. I was in the town's bookshop and had just been looking at the one well-handled copy of my novel on the shelves, and there he was. Not having written a word in months, the symbolism wasn't lost on me.

To begin with I wasn't that worried about my inability to write. I'd just come off the back of a very long and complicated project, written amidst a very stressful period of my life, and the very thought of writing another word was something I just couldn't stomach. So, having used up all my creative energies, I decided that a decent-sized break away from my desk was in order to catch up with things: friends, chores, sleep – basically life in general. And, apart from the odd idea occurring to me which I duly scribbled down, I found that I didn't miss writing at all. But after two weeks of idleness, I decided that the time had come to sit back down at my desk with the ideas I'd accumulated and start again. Only when I did there was nothing there.

Absolutely nothing.

Perturbed, but not overly so, I realised that I needed a little longer, and a week or so later tried again – but with the same lack of success. Only this time it started to get to me. So, with some reluctance I gave it a bit longer before trying again. But, finding it increasingly difficult to fill all that dead time with anything satisfying, I found myself back at my desk sooner than I'd planned, only to get up two hours later with nothing to show for it except a creeping feeling of panic that maybe this wasn't a short-term problem after all.

That night I didn't sleep well, laying for hours trying to reason it out. Unable to accept the idea that I was through, or that even more time away from my desk was the solution, I clung onto the thought that at least I kept having *ideas*. I knew I must still have the creative urge, and it was just a matter of finding the right way to get it started again. So, the next morning I sat down at my desk and drew up a list of possible ways that I might break the deadlock. With the time on my hands to see it through, I decided to spend at least a day on each different approach until I found one that worked for me. And believe me, I tried. I tried every trick I could think of.

I tried relaxing into it. I tried hitting the ground running. I tried writing what I knew, what I was good at. I tried writing in styles and genres I wouldn't normally write in. I tried writing what I felt. I tried telling myself it didn't matter how long it took as long as it happened, then that it had to be done *now* while the ideas were fresh in my mind. I tried to convince myself that it wasn't a big deal and that given some of the problems in the world, I should be thoroughly ashamed of worrying about it all so much. I sat at my desk for days on end, and when that didn't work, I tried spending as much time away from it as possible, settling down in the library and coffee shops with paper and pen. I walked for miles around the town, park and shopping centres, looking for places to sit or stand, armed with nothing but a well-charged phone. Still nothing. As the panic and frustration began to turn into anger, I tried leaving the house empty handed, hoping to somehow trick my brain into action and send me rushing to the nearest stationers for the pen and paper I'd need to scrawl down the torrent of ideas that would surely follow; and when that didn't work and the anger began to burn itself out and be replaced by shock, I admitted defeat.

Unsure what to do next but certain I couldn't put myself through that again, I struggled to find things to occupy me, eventually ending up doing all the little jobs I'd been putting off for months, including – ironically – moving a load of my old manuscripts into the loft. After heaving the last, particularly heavy box upstairs, I flopped down in front of the TV and flicked through the channels. I briefly caught what looked like an advert for holidays in Australia, and no sooner had the image of the Sydney Opera House appeared on the screen than I suddenly remembered what happened to me over there and wondered if a similar thing might not be happening again.

When I was nineteen, in between jobs and with no ties, I was fortunate enough to be able to visit the various friends and relatives I had in Australia for a couple of months; and because none of them would take a penny off me in board and lodgings, even more fortunate to be able to spend a week in Los Angeles on the way. After a wonderful, dizzying week in California, I headed Down Under filled with excitement. But when I got there the strangest thing happened: for the first twelve days I was there, I couldn't eat anything. Not only that, but the idea, the very *concept* of eating itself seemed utterly alien to me. Later of course I put it down to jetlag and lack of sleep, excitement, my body and mind rebelling in some strange way against the huge changes I'd undergone in the space of a week; but at the time it was worrying to say the least. I remembered one day in particular about five days in a plate of food being put in front of me, and thinking how odd it was that I was supposed to put the objects on the plate into my mouth, chew and then swallow them. At the time eating what was on that plate made about as much sense as eating the chair I was sitting on, or the plate itself; I felt like I was being asked to do something that was utterly alien to my nature. And as these memories swept through my mind, I realised that I now felt the same way about writing: not only could I *not* write, but the very idea of it was so strange it was as if I'd never done it in the first place; only unlike the experience in Australia, this time it wasn't going to end. Alarmed at the very thought, I tried to reason against it, remembering once more the ideas I'd kept having; only to be hit with the thought that they weren't ideas at all, were nothing more than leftover thoughts, imagined itchings from a limb long since amputated, echoes from a life that no longer existed.

Stunned by these revelations and with time weighing even more heavily on me than before, I did the only thing I could do in the circumstances, namely try and get on with things as normally as possible. I went for walks, did my shopping, read a bit (strictly as a reader I noticed, not with one eye on the writing as used to happen), did the housework; by and large I kept myself busy. Beneath it all was a dull feeling of emptiness, yet even then a tiny sliver of optimism remained. And so, when one day I realised I hadn't been to the local bookshop for a while, I headed for the back of the store with the vague hope that someone might've bought the single copy of my novel that was in stock, giving me at least a little encouragement. Not completely surprised to see it still there but disappointed nevertheless, I touched its cracked spine for a second and then turned round. And that's when I saw myself, talking to the assistant at the cash register.

Of course, at first, I thought it wasn't me, just someone wearing the same kind of coat. But then I saw it wasn't just the coat, it was the trousers and shoes as well; then I realised that the glasses were the same, and the hair, right down to the streaks of grey at the sides. But what really clinched it was the body language, something I can't say I'd even noticed before – I mean, who's aware of their body language unless it's pointed out to them? But the little movements and gestures I was seeing now *felt* so much like mine that I started to feel uncomfortable looking at them. Then, after a quick glance down at the floor, I saw myself smile slightly, nod at the assistant and walk out of the shop.

For a moment I couldn't move – my heart was beating so heavily it felt like it was swelling up inside my chest – but eventually I managed to push past the few people in my way and out into the street. Only by the time I got there, ridiculous as it sounds, I wasn't there anymore.

For days afterwards I tried to put this event into some kind of rational context, but beyond the obvious symbolism of an author who couldn't write just happening to see himself in a shop full of books or – god help me – taking it as a weird sign that I was meant to write after all, I got nowhere. Nevertheless, on a couple of occasions when I returned to town, I had to stop myself from entering the bookshop; the first time with the idea that I might see myself again, the second with the half-baked notion of engaging the shop assistant in conversation to try and ascertain what the conversation had been about. But after a week or so these intense speculations, rational and otherwise, slowly began to fade, replaced once again by the numbed confusion I was slowly getting used to.

Which meant when it happened again a few weeks later I was no more prepared than I'd been the first time.

I was barely aware it was happening at all until it was almost over. I'd just finished doing my shopping, and rather than walk home had decided to get the bus. Paying the driver, I'd just started tearing my ticket from the machine when I heard a voice behind me say:

"I've no idea where they come from – I'm not sure I'd want to know either. You can say it's a mixture of things you think and feel and what's going on around you, but when you get down to it, it's really a mystery."

Looking round with a start as the doors were closing behind me, I turned just in time to see the back of a small man's head before it was obscured by the bus shelter as we sped away.

The fact that I couldn't say for sure it was *physically* me didn't matter; I recognised my flat tones from the message on my answer machine plainly enough. But it was hearing those words that really got their hooks in me, words that I'd heard myself say many times over the years in response to the age-old question all writers get asked: *Where do you get your ideas from?*

Stunned, I stumbled towards the nearest seat and slumped down.

Over the next four months or so I saw myself – or rather 'him' as I started to think of him – several times whilst out and about on my travels, usually on crowded streets or too far away for me to get near him. These unnerving little moments aside I carried on as best as I could, trying to adapt to a life that now often felt like little more than a series of daydreams that were happening to someone else, my occasional sessions at my desk conducted with a less little enthusiasm each time, each one shorter than the last.

It was at the end of one of these sessions that I noticed the calendar above my desk, now several months behind, just as I was about to turn out the light. Flipping the pages to the correct month, I was surprised to see the following weekend's squares ringed in blue biro. After a few seconds' confusion I remembered the reason: the annual writers' convention I went to without fail every year and had booked at the start of the year to guarantee a place.

Shocked that I'd forgotten about it, I wondered if I should go. I certainly didn't feel like it – part of the reason I'd forgotten about it in the first place was because I hadn't kept in touch with anyone who'd be going – but eventually I decided to make the effort. Perhaps being among like-minded people would reignite some spark within me, and god knows I needed the break. Besides, it was too late to cancel. So, packing a few things the following Friday, I sauntered over to the train station paying full fare because I hadn't booked the tickets in advance; a few hours later after somehow avoiding anyone I knew on the way in, I sat on the bed in my hotel room trying to pluck up the courage to go downstairs. Eventually, realising the only place I was going to find that courage was in a pint glass, I left my room and headed for the heart of any convention: the bar.

As is usual at such events I heard where it was before I saw it, its pumps and optics obscured by a chattering throng of people four deep. Before I had a chance to single out anyone in particular, I heard someone call my name maybe ten feet or so away and saw a few of the friends I've made over the years wedged into a corner beside a wooden pillar. Oddly relieved yet also apprehensive to see them after such a long absence, I put on my best smile and squeezed my way through the crowd towards them.

We'd been chatting for about twenty minutes when I saw him. He was squashed in at the bar with a pint glass in his hand, talking to people I'd seen around but never really spoken to. I couldn't hear much of what he was saying given the general noise in the place, but I caught the odd bit, something about the need to keep plugging away no matter what. Seeing the empty glasses around me and using a lull in our conversation as my cue, I asked everyone what they wanted and did my best to worm my way through the bodies towards the bar; but by the time I got to where he'd been standing the only thing there was a gap. Pausing momentarily before filling it, I was grateful the barmaid was at the other end of the bar, my drinks order temporarily lost to me.

What with the constant whirl of panels and book launches, the almost non-stop conversation and the copious amounts of alcohol that went with it all, I only spotted him once after that. But I did hear him a few times as I zipped about, extolling the virtues of a creative life, and to be fair sounding like he knew what he was talking about. In that he wasn't alone, because so did pretty much everybody else I spoke to that weekend. But unlike everybody else who seemed to be enthused and energised by what was going on, I felt as empty as when I'd arrived; almost as bad was the feeling that any kinship, any *connection* I had with those around me was also draining away. So, by the time it got to Sunday and the sad, protracted series of goodbyes that began after breakfast as people returned to their regular lives, I was ready for it to end; but at the same time the prospect of returning to what was now *my* regular life didn't exactly appeal either. Opting for something between these two positions, I hung around until lunchtime with the idea of going for a walk, grabbing something to eat and then heading off.

Glad of the fresh air after the stuffiness of the hotel, my head cleared sufficiently for me to remember I was running short of money. Heading in the general direction of the cash machine I'd seen on Friday en-route to the hotel, I turned right into a side street, finding it lined with cobbles. Realising I'd taken a wrong turn I was just about to retrace my steps when I saw him about halfway down, standing in the road, alone.

Unable to believe I was so close, my heart beat even harder than it had in the bookshop, my breathing so loud I tried to quieten it, afraid he'd run if he sensed I was near; but instead he just stood there, untroubled, idly looking along the street whilst I frantically tried to figure out what to do. Then, as he glanced down at his cheap digital watch – *my* cheap digital watch – my body made the decision for me.

Running in a way I hadn't since childhood and not caring about the noise, I hurtled towards him along the cobbles so fast I could barely see, knowing this time I was going to reach him, somehow keeping my balance until I'd covered the distance, then losing it and clattering to the ground and raising myself on my hands and knees to turn and look at him, as ragged breaths tore from my body.

Only to find nothing there.

#

So that's my story. It's not a particularly sad story in the context of the world, or one told to elicit sympathy or as some psychological double-bluff to get things moving again. If that was the case, I'd have written it months ago. A couple of times in the past when I've had writer's block, I've written stories about it that have helped me break free of it. But this time I'm writing about it because, apparently, it's the only story I have left, or for that matter am able to tell. No, the reason I've put off writing it for so long is that I wanted to be sure first – and now that I am, not only does it feel like the right time to tell it, it feels like it might be the *only* time, because even though I still see him around it's not nearly with the same frequency, and every time he's that little bit further away from me. But on the rare occasions I do spot him, I head back to my desk and try and come up with something, only for it always to end the same way. Sometimes, when I get up from the desk my gaze falls on my bookshelves; or more specifically, the two shelves at the top filled with copies of my books. But instead of the feelings of pride, warmth and disbelief that I used to feel, only a form of the latter remains; the happy disbelief I used to feel on seeing the fruits of my labour replaced by the overwhelming feeling that I haven't written these books at all, that I'd somehow amassed a series of books written by someone with the same name as me so I could foolishly bask in their success. Turning away with something approaching shame and a bewilderment that I can't put into words, I try in vain to tell myself that I'm not walking away from writing, or that writing has walked away from me – if it was as simple as that I could catch up with it. But for the time being at least there doesn't seem to be any point in me trying to run after it.

But if it wants to run into me, it knows where I am.

Called 'a writer of considerable energy' in *The Encyclopedia of Science Fiction*, John Travis is the author of four books—a short story collection, *Mostly Monochrome Stories*, and two weird crime novels, *The Terror and the Tortoiseshell* and *The Designated Coconut*, the former attracting the attention of several Hollywood film companies. Also, available as an ebook and shortly to appear in paperback, the Crime/Horror/Fairytale hybrid *Greenbeard*.

Published nearly eighty times, his many short stories and novellas have appeared in anthologies and journals such as *Nemonymous*, *The Urbanite*, *At Ease with the Dead*, *All Hallows*, *Supernatural Tales*, *British Invasion*, *The Monster Book for Girls*, *Horror Without Victims*, *Terror Tales of Northwest England* and in both volumes of *The Humdrumming Books of Horror Stories*, his story from the second volume, 'The Tobacconist's Concession' appearing on the 2009 shortlist for a British Fantasy Award.

He's also had his work praised by TED Klein and David Renwick, and had an invisible poem read out on Radio 1 by John Hegley. A second full-length collection, *Gaseous Clay and Other Ambivalent Tales*, is forthcoming from Eibonvale Press. A third crime novel and a further collection of short stories remained unpublished, looking for homes.

Living mostly in his head but occasionally venturing beyond it, his undersized physical form resides in the north of England.

His Facebook page is:

www.facebook.com/JohnTravisWriter